Batman Can't Fly

Batman Can't Fly

DAVID HINES

faber and faber

First published in 1997
by Faber and Faber Limited
3 Queen Square London WC1N 3AU

Photoset by Avon Dataset Ltd, Warwickshire
Printed and bound in Great Britain by
Mackays of Chatham plc, Chatham, Kent

All rights reserved

© David Hines, 1997

David Hines is hereby identified as author of this
work in accordance with Section 77 of the Copyright,
Designs and Patents Act 1988

*This book is sold subject to the condition that it shall not,
by way of trade or otherwise, be lent, resold, hired out or
otherwise circulated without the publisher's prior consent in
any form of binding or cover other than that in which it is
published and without a similar condition including this
condition being imposed on the subsequent purchaser*

A CIP record for this book
is available from the British Library

ISBN 0-571-17565-1

10 9 8 7 6 5 4 3 2 1

For Caterina

'Who are you talking to?'

'Nobody,' I said, looking up at my mother and starting to blush. 'I was only playing.'

'Well, get up. Just look at your shorts, they're filthy. Come here.' She turned me around and brushed the dirt off. 'These were clean on this morning, now look at them. There, that's better.'

I tried to get away but she held on to my arm.

'What's this?' She pulled at my cloak.

'I'm Batman,' I said, and turned to show it off.

'Curtains? Don't let your gran catch you.'

'She said I could have this one; she was only going to use it for dusters.'

'That's all right then.'

It was summer and I'm sure it was the afternoon because our house was in shadow and the opposite side of the street was sunny. My mother leaned back against the garden wall and looked down the street to the main road.

I waited for her to go. I don't think I'd ever seen her in the garden before. My grandmother did all the gardening and I helped.

'Are you waiting for somebody?' I asked.

'Nope,' she said, popping the 'p'. 'Are you?'

A car went by and tooted; my mother waved.

'Do you know him?'

'Look at these weeds,' my mother said. 'Come on, let's do some weeding and surprise your gran when she gets back. You start at that end; I'll start over here. I know, we'll have a race.'

'What are we going to put them in?'

'What?'

'Gran always puts them in a bucket.'

'We don't need a bucket. Put them on the path and we'll sweep them up after.'

It was quicker to use both hands and to collect a handful before dropping them on the path, but my mother picked and dropped them one at a time.

'*And the days grow short when they reach September* . . .' my mother sang softly to herself.

'I'm winning,' I said.

'How can you tell?'

'That white rose there, that's the middle and I'm nearer than you are.'

She began to sing again. '*And the days dwindle down to a precious few* . . .'

'Mum . . .'

'That's my name. What?'

'Why do we live with Gran instead of in our own house?'

'Because I like it here. I've always lived here.'

'But you're always rowing with Gran.'

'That's different,' she said. 'I've won.' And she stood up.

'But you've left all those.' I walked over to take a closer look. 'There . . .' I pointed. 'Look at all those weeds you've left.'

'They're not weeds, they're flowers.'

'No, they're not,' I said, and pulled out a weed and held it up. 'And look at my pile, loads more than yours.'

'I'm having a break then,' she said, and rested her elbows on the garden wall again.

'When's Gran coming back?' I asked, scraping the

weeds into a pile. 'Mum, what time's Gran coming back? Mum, Mum . . .'

'What?'

'What time is she coming back?'

'How should I know? Sometime tonight. Late.' And she began to sing again: '*And I haven't got time for the waiting game* . . . Don't you like living with your gran? You should . . . you don't know how lucky you are. Your gran spoils you.' She turned to look at me: 'She loves you more than she loved any of us.' It sounded like a threat. 'That's why she dresses you up and takes you everywhere. You're her little pet, you can get anything you want out of your gran, but money's not everything.' She looked away. 'It's easy to put your hand in your pocket when you have money, but love, that's a different thing. You're better off with your gran.'

She clasped her hands behind her neck and pushed her head backwards. 'I could stretch for a mile if it wasn't for coming back.'

'Mum . . . why don't you want to come on holiday with us?'

'Who says I don't?'

'Gran says you don't want to come . . . Why?'

'I don't like the seaside. Besides, I haven't got anything to wear.'

'You've got hundreds of dresses.'

'New, I mean.'

'I've got nearly ten pounds saved. You can have that.'

My mother didn't often smile, but when she did it was a beautiful smile, and just then I would have died for another one.

'It's my holiday money; it's in a secret place. Do you want to know where?'

'Better not tell me, or I'll be off.'

'Where would you go?'

'I don't know... on a slow boat to China.'

'Can I come with you?' But she didn't answer.

'Mum, if you could choose ... Mum ...'

'What?'

'If you could choose ... Mum, are you listening?'

'Yes. What?'

'If you could choose to be invisible, or to be able to fly, which would you choose?'

'Fly,' she said, looking up at the sky. 'I'm already half invisible.'

'Batman can fly,' I said.

'No, he can't. Superman can.'

'No, Batman too,' I insisted. 'Shall I show you?'

'Go on then,' she said, 'show me.'

I ran upstairs to my grandmother's bedroom. I slid open the window and stepped out on to the top of the bay window.

'Look, Mum ...' I shouted.

It seemed twice as far looking down. I didn't really think I could fly, but I was sure that if I held the corners of my cloak I could parachute into the garden.

'Go on then, jump,' my mother shouted.

In my imagination I saw myself glide down and land at my mother's feet.

'Do you want me to?'

'Yes, if you're going to jump, jump.'

'Really?'

'Yes.'

I took a deep breath and jumped.

'I think he's knocked himself out,' I heard a man's voice say.

'Turn him over,' my mother said.

Uncle Mike and my mother were looking at me. I felt as if I was being crushed under a sheet of glass. 'I can't breathe, I can't breathe,' I said, and tried to push them away.

'Lift him up,' my mother said.

They sat me up and rested my back against the garden wall.

'No bones broken?' Uncle Mike squeezed my arms. I shook my head.

'What were you doing?'

'Climbing,' my mother said.

'You were lucky not to break your neck,' he said, 'You would have if you hadn't landed in the roses. Look, you've flattened them.'

'I don't know what your gran will say,' my mother said, pulling the thorns and crushed roses from my jumper. 'Look at your clothes: ruined.'

'Leave him alone, never mind about that. Let's see if he can stand; you hold his arm. Easy does it.'

It felt like a nail was being hammered into my shin and I started to cry. They sat me down again.

'I think it's broken,' my uncle said.

'You're a fine one,' my mother said. 'I told you Batman couldn't fly.'

'What?' Uncle Mike asked, but he didn't wait for an answer. 'Come on, I'll take him to the hospital. Help me carry him to the car. He can lay on the back seat.'

My mother was just about to shut the door when Mrs Hawksmoor stopped and peered in at me. 'Has he had an accident?' she asked my mother.

'Well,' my mother said, 'sort of.'

'What happened?'

'A lion attacked him,' my mother said as if it happened all the time. I looked at my mother.

'A lion?' Mrs Hawksmoor said, stepping backwards and nearly falling over. 'A lion?'

'Just now, in the garden,' my mother said. 'I had to hit it with my shoe; it wouldn't let go of his leg.'

'I think you're pulling mine,' Mrs Hawksmoor said.

'No, it's true,' my mother said, looking hurt. 'It escaped from the circus this morning.'

'Look, can we get going?' Uncle Mike said, leaning out of the car.

'Yes, I'm coming,' my mother said.

'I've got to get to work, you know,' Uncle Mike said, revving up the engine.

'I'd better go and get my washing in,' Mrs Hawksmoor said before she turned and walked quickly away up the street.

'Here we are,' Uncle Mike said, switching off the engine. He turned to look at me and asked if I was all right.

'Yes, thank you,' I said, and tried to force a smile.

They got out of the car and walked to the back. They stopped when they met.

'Tonight,' my uncle Mike said.

'Not now,' my mother said and tried to get past him, but he grabbed her arm and stopped her.

'I'll come around for you,' he said and pulled my mother a few steps away from the car, but I could still hear them through the open window.

'About nine o'clock.'

'Not tonight,' my mother said, 'not now, how can I?'

'I'll wait for you then . . .' he said. 'Usual place.'

'I'll see,' my mother said. 'I'll see.'

'I'll wait for you,' my uncle persisted. 'Don't let me down, do you hear? At nine.'

'I'll see,' my mother said softly.

'Nine,' my uncle hissed.

'I said I'll see,' my mother said in a hard whisper.

When they opened the car door my mother's face was white but my uncle's was red.

'Bring out your dead,' my mother chanted as my uncle carried me into the hospital like a baby.

'I'll have to get back to work,' my uncle said, sitting me down on a chair. 'Don't forget,' he said and looked straight at my mother.

After my leg had been X-rayed, we waited in a small room. I counted the ticks of the clock; exactly sixty for the red second hand to go round, a short buzz, and the minute hand took another step forward.

We didn't speak, I just counted, and my mother looked as if she was trying to outstare a fire extinguisher.

'There you are,' the doctor said as if he was surprised to see us. 'Good news,' and he smiled at me. 'We won't be chopping your leg off. Not today, anyway.'

I suppose he thought he was being funny.

'No, it's fine,' he said and came over to have a look at me. 'It's not broken, it's a greenstick fracture.'

'A what what fracture?' my mother said, giving in to the fire extinguisher.

'Greenstick,' he said, and went on to explain. 'It's quite common with children. You see, their bones are soft, not brittle like grown-ups'.'

My mother laughed, she often laughed at the strangest things, and it seemed to put the doctor off. Then he started again.

'So when they have a fall their bones don't always break; they just bend and crack a little. We'll still have to put his leg in plaster for a few weeks.'

'A few weeks?' I said. 'What about my holidays?'

'It shouldn't stop you going on holiday,' he said, 'but I wouldn't go swimming,' and he laughed. 'And we would like to keep him in overnight.'

'But I haven't brought his pyjamas,' my mum said.

'We can kit him out; besides, it's only for one night. He's had a nasty fall and we would like to keep an eye on him, just to be sure, you know.'

'Well, if you say so,' my mother said and stood up. 'Is that clock right?' The doctor checked his watch and said it was.

'You don't have to stay, I'll be all right,' I said to make it easier for her, but she waited for the doctor.

'Yes, that's fine,' he said.

'I'll come and see you tonight then,' she said, gathering up my clothes. 'Mustn't forget these.'

'Leave my cloak.'

'What for?'

'I want it,' I said.

'Thinks he can fly,' my mum said to the doctor.

'Please, Mum . . .'

'But it's dirty. Look,' and she held it up. Seeing the clock again settled it. 'Oh, all right then, I'll see you tonight.'

'I have to take this to reception,' the doctor said, closing my file. 'I'll walk down with you.'

As they left my mum slipped her arm into his and gave me an exaggerated wink.

The ward was full of visitors.

'Do you want anything?' a nurse asked me, but I just

shook my head. 'Aren't you having any visitors tonight?'

'Yes,' I said, sitting up, 'my mum's coming . . . my gran would come too but she's visiting my aunty Enid.'

'Well, she'll have to get a move on,' and the nurse glanced at her watch. 'There isn't much time left; the bell goes at eight.'

When the bell rang, I closed my eyes and pretended to be asleep.

Here he co-o-omes, that's Cathy's clown . . .

I don't know how the Everley Brothers knew about me and Cathy Eastwood, but there they were again on the radio.

I was sitting underneath the kitchen window playing with a money-spider.

You know a man can't crawl . . .

It was the first time I was in love.

La, la, la, la, he's gotta stand tall . . .

Cathy was new at school and I couldn't stop thinking about her. I used to lie in bed at night and stretch my arms out and pretend to hold her.

I knew she liked me; the only problem was, I was still going out with Josephine Towers. But every night after school, after I'd walked Josephine home, I used to run through St Paul's Churchyard just to walk the last few streets with Cathy.

I'd asked her out loads of times, but she always said the same thing: 'What about Josephine?' So yesterday I'd told her I'd finished with Josephine and tonight we're going to the pictures.

Every time I dropped the money-spider it made a fine thread. I wanted to see how long it would take before it ran out, but it was beginning to get on my nerves.

'What are you doing?'

I turned around. My mother was standing in the door-way.

'I've got this money-spider. Look,' I said. But when I held up my hand to show her, it had gone.

'I've been watching you. Don't wave your arms around like that,' she said, walking down the steps, 'people will think you're spastic or something.'

She closed her eyes and held back her head for the sun. 'I can hear the sea,' she whispered. 'Listen.'

My mother had only been back a few days. I'd stopped asking where she went a long time ago. She was a reddish golden colour, so wherever it was this time, it must have been sunny.

She was wearing white shoes, white skirt and a sort of sailor top with a square navy blue collar.

'Where are you going?' I asked.

'Along a soft pink beach,' she answered in one slow breath and smiled at the 'view'.

'No,' I said, 'I mean . . . really, where are you going?'

'Out. Come on; you're coming with me.'

'I can't, I'm going swimming.'

'Well, who's stopping you? We won't be long.'

We nearly missed the bus, but Mum shouted and waved. She could do a loud whistle too, but she knew it embar-rassed me. The bus stopped.

'You look well,' said the bus conductor to my mum and pressed against the seat in front making it creak.

'I've just come back from the south of France,' my mum said.

Everybody in the bus turned round and stared.

'It's all right for some,' he said, and dropped the tickets

on her lap. 'Why didn't you send me a postcard then?'

'I was going to, but I couldn't remember your wife's name,' and she gave him one of her silly smiles.

After he'd moved away, I tried again. 'Where are we going?'

'To see somebody.'

'Who?'

'A man about a dog.'

That's what she always said when she didn't want to tell me anything.

When we got off the bus, Mum took a piece of paper out of her bag. 'We can walk from here.'

'Walk?' I said, pulling away. 'Walk?'

'It's not far,' she said, taking hold of my hand. 'It won't kill you.' She looked at the paper again and said more to herself than to me, 'According to this, it should be just around the corner.'

'Mum, you said it wasn't far; this is miles.'

'There it is,' she said. 'Shut up.' We crossed the road. 'This is it; we want sixty-four.'

'Who are we going to see?'

'A friend,' my mum said. 'No; these are odd this side, we want even . . . come on, nearly there.'

'What friend?' I asked.

'A friend . . . a woman I met at work . . .'

I couldn't remember my mother ever having had a job, unless she'd had one on the quiet and hadn't told anybody. My gran was always saying that my mum was very secretive, like a spy; actually, what she said was that my mum couldn't stop telling lies, but I suppose that's what she meant.

'Here it is: sixty-four,' my mum said, and rang the bell.

'There's nobody in,' I said. 'Look at the curtains . . . Come on, let's go.'

She rang the bell again. 'Who's there?' a voice said from behind the closed door.

'Sylvia,' my mum said.

'Sylvia?' I repeated and looked at my mum. I could never get used to all her names. An old woman opened the door.

'Hello, love,' she said. 'Come in.' She didn't look at me. 'He can wait in there,' she said, opening the door of the front room and switching on the light. I felt as if I'd got something catching.

The room was as hot as the boiler room at school, and the thick velvet curtains made it feel like night. On the mantelpiece was a mortar shell made into a clock. Everything was polished and stood to attention.

There was a sculpture of a naked woman on the sideboard; her hands were tied and she held them up as if she was praying. I had a closer look and tapped it; it was metal, a dark coppery colour except for the breasts; the tips were as shiny as new pennies. I touched them and sat down. Should have brought a comic, I thought, and looked at my watch: it was half past ten.

I heard the water being turned on and a bang in the pipes when it was turned off. I got off the chair and opened the curtains; most of the houses had their windows open. These windows looked as though they had never been opened. There was the sound of water again . . . I waited for the bang. I sat down again and closed my eyes. A door being slammed woke me up. I looked at my watch; it was nearly twelve o'clock.

'Where is she?' I said, stamping my feet to get rid of the pins and needles. I carefully opened the door and looked up the stairs and listened. All I could hear was the clock in the hallway slowly ticking; then I heard them coming downstairs.

'Well, you know where I am,' I heard the old woman say just before I closed the door. 'There he is,' the old woman said, poking her head around the door. My mum was standing behind her; she looked pale, but perhaps it was just the light.

'Do you like sweeties?' the old woman asked me, pretending to smile. I looked at the squashed and fluff-covered toffees and shook my head.

'No, thank you; I don't like sweets.'

'Who is she?' I asked Mum when we got into the street.

'A dressmaker. Come on, never mind about her,' and she put her arm around my shoulder. 'Let's go home.'

It wasn't the light; she was pale and shivering. We just missed the bus, so we got a taxi. The driver started talking straight away, but my mum didn't say a word; she just closed her eyes and let the wind (the tropical wind?) cool her lovely face.

When we got home Philip Heath was waiting. 'The others have gone,' he said. 'I said I'd wait for you.'

'I'll go and get my swimming things,' I said.

'Can you lend me the money to get in?' he said and pulled me back.

'You're always on the scrounge, Heath.'

'I'll give it back to you on Saturday when I get my spendo.'

'You'd better,' I said and followed my mum to the door.

I was waiting for her to get her key out when I saw the patch of blood on the back of her skirt. 'Mum,' I said, 'look,' and I pointed.

When we got inside she closed the door and looked.

'What a mess,' she said. 'I'd better soak it or it will never come out.' The look on my face must have frightened her. 'It's all right; don't worry, it's nothing.' I watched her walk slowly up the stairs. 'And you be careful,' she said without turning around, 'I don't want you acting the goat on those diving boards.'

'No, I won't, I promise.'

She stopped on the landing and looked at me. I wanted her to say 'stay with me', but she didn't. 'I know you; you can't help showing off, especially if there are any girls there.'

'I won't; honest.'

Phil and I ran all the way to the park but I stopped when I saw Cathy Eastwood talking to Josephine Towers. 'Come on,' I said to Phil, 'I'll show you a short cut to the Lido.'

Mr Philips the milkman was laughing as he came out by the back door; that meant my mum was up.

'Hello,' he said, 'your mum should be on the telly.'

When I went into the kitchen my mum was emptying the tea-pot into the sink.

'Gran says you shouldn't do that,' I said, 'that's how it gets blocked.'

She ran the cold water. 'She'll never know,' she said, looking over her shoulder at me, 'will she?'

'Mr Philips says you should be on the telly.'

My mum laughed and put two striped mugs into the sink.

'You should, you know,' I said, kneeling on the fender and warming my hands by the fire. 'Everybody says so.' I looked at her. 'Why don't you?'

She unwound the towel from her wet hair. 'No,' she said, leaning forward and rubbing it.

'Why not? Don't you think you're good enough?'

She turned the towel over to find a dry place. 'I'm too good,' and started rubbing her hair again.

'Too good?' I said. The fire was making my fingers ache. 'How can you be too good?' She straightened up and tied the towel into a turban. 'How?' I said, but she didn't answer. She wiped the steam from the small mirror by the sink and stared at herself. 'How?' I asked again.

'You'll see,' she said.

I turned my head from side to side and let the fire warm my face. 'Where's Gran?' I said, but my mum was lost in her own reflection. 'Mum, where's Gran? Mum . . . '

'What,' she snapped and made me jump. 'Mum, Mum; I'm going to change my name.'

'Well, that's not unusual,' I said standing up and sucking my throbbing fingers. 'Has she gone out?'

'She?' my mum said, turning away from the mirror. 'Who's she? The cat next door?'

'Gran,' I said.

'Well, say Gran then.'

'I did; where is she?'

'Gone shoplifting with your aunty Enid.' I looked at her. 'How do I know,' she said, looking out of the window and up to the sky. 'Your friend Cigar is here.'

I pulled back the curtains; he was looking over the wall. When he saw me he pretended to shoot but he missed by a mile.

'He's not right in the head, that one,' my mum said, rinsing the two mugs and putting them on the draining board.

'He's all right,' I said, reloading. 'He's one of my best friends.'

'Well, if he's one of your best I wouldn't like to meet your worst.'

'He's all right,' I said, lobbing a hand grenade at him. 'Have we got anything to eat?' I said, looking inside the fridge.

'Your gran will be back soon,' my mum said. 'I saw him in town yesterday.'

'Who?' I said, looking in the fridge.

'Who?' my mum said. 'Who are we talking about? Micky Mouse?'

'Did you?' I said, cutting a piece of cheese and closing the fridge door. 'Who was he with? Pluto?'

'Your friend Cigar,' she said.

'Agar,' I said. 'His name's Agar.'

'Well, whatever his name is, he's cracked.'

'I know he is,' I said, 'that's why I like him; he's different.'

'Eat some bread with it,' my mum said, watching me in the small mirror. 'Do you know what he was doing? He was standing outside Kirklea market holding a white stick and pretending to be blind, and asking people to take him across the zebra crossing.'

'I know; it was a dare,' I said, finishing the cheese.

'Pretending to be blind?' My mum looked at me, then out of the window. 'Look at him.' She lifted the curtains and tapped on the window. 'Get off the wall,' she shouted, 'right off.' Agar slid off, then stroked and patted the top of the wall. 'And you say he's all right,' my mum said, letting the curtains fall back.

'I'm going carolling with him tonight; he knows some great places,' I said.

'I can imagine.' She was back at the mirror again.

It was three days before Christmas and soon the house would be full of uncles, aunts and cousins. My aunty Enid and uncle Mike always came first. Aunty Enid helped my gran with the shopping and the baking.

'Where's Uncle Mike?' I asked.

'Still in bed, I suppose,' my mum said, nudging me from in front of the fire. 'Move over.'

'What's my aunty Enid got me for Christmas?' I asked, trying to open a packet of chocolate biscuits.

'Don't open them,' my mum said.

'I only want one,' I said, trying to get my thumb nail behind the silver foil flap.

'Your gran says they're for Christmas.'

I got one out. 'Dark chocolate? I hate dark chocolate,' I said.

'Talk to the wall,' my mum said.

'Hello wall, want to see a trick? See this chocolate biscuit?' And I put it in my mouth. 'Now you don't.'

'Mad,' my mum said, and lifted the back of her skirt to warm her legs. 'I don't feel like going out now, you know. No more,' and she snatched the packet from me and put it in the cupboard.

'So what did my aunty Enid get me?' I asked again.

'Nothing,' my mum said with her mouth full of chocolate biscuit. 'She says you're too old,' and she took up sentry duty in front of the fire.

'I'm not,' I protested, but I knew she was only joking. My aunty Enid and uncle Mike didn't have any children and my aunty really liked me. She was always buying me things, not just for my birthday or at Christmas.

'I'm off then,' I said and walked over to the door.

'Not far I hope,' my mum said.

'No. Billy's got a new air rifle,' I said. 'I won't be long.'

'Do me a favour,' my mum said.

I turned around; she had her big favour eyes in. I just stared back and waited for it.

'Come here,' she said, 'and I'll whisper it to you.' She held me by the arms, then whispered: 'Make the beds.'

'Mum,' I tried to get away.

'Go on,' she said. 'I'll give you something.'

'What?' I said and stopped struggling.

'A kiss,' she said.

'A kiss?'

'All right then,' she said, 'two kisses,' and she got me

with two wet kisses on both cheeks. 'Now you owe me,' she said and let go.

I wiped the kisses on the back of my hand. 'I don't want your kisses,' I said, finishing off with the tea towel.

'There are plenty that do,' she said.

'Well, you can give them to them; see if I care.'

'Go on; it won't take you long,' she said.

'Or you,' I said, jumping up to see my face in the mirror.

'I could make you.' My mum always kept her threats.

'Oh yeah,' I said, feeling brave with my hand on the door knob. 'How?'

'Smell this,' my mum held up her fist. 'You're not too big for a smack and besides I haven't given you your Christmas present yet.' She looked serious: 'I'll give it to the first kid I meet in the street.' My mum had done things like that before. 'Can I do the beds when I come back?' I said. 'I won't be long. Honest.'

'Before your gran gets back,' my mum agreed. 'You know what she's like.'

'Don't go,' I said and walked over to the fire. 'Stay here.' I tried to hold her hand but she pulled it away.

'Don't be such a baby,' she mocked.

'Why do you always go away at Christmas?' I asked and tried to hold her hand again.

'Christmas is for families,' she said and went back to the small mirror.

'Aren't we family?' I said, following her.

'You know what I mean, I'm like a red rag to a bull.' She looked at me. 'You know that, don't you? And however hard I try, there're always arguments; they won't leave me alone.'

'Well, don't argue back,' I said, 'and I'll stand up for you.'

She smiled. 'No, it's better if I'm not here.'

'Where are you going?' I asked.

'To stay with a friend . . . nothing special,' she said.

'Who?'

'Somebody.'

'Who?'

'Nobody you know.'

'So tell me then.'

'You don't know them.'

'Is it a man?'

She didn't answer.

'It is, isn't it?'

'Does it matter?'

'Who is he?'

'I could tell you any name and you still wouldn't know.'

'Don't go,' I said and tried to hold her hand but she pulled it away. 'Stay with me.'

'Stop being a baby,' she said. 'Anyway, I've promised now.'

Agar squeezed his face against the window; we both turned to look at him.

'Go on then, go,' my mum said and pushed me. 'And don't forget the beds.' I waited for a few seconds but I knew she wasn't going to change her mind.

When I got back I could hear the shouting before I opened the kitchen door; then I remembered the beds. I was going to run but I was starving. I needed an excuse so I limped into the kitchen. My gran was standing by the sink; she was wearing her hat and overcoat and holding two full shopping bags.

'All right then, that's enough now,' my gran said when she saw me. My mum and my aunty Enid were standing at opposite ends of the kitchen table staring at each other with faces like a pair of mad dogs. Then I noticed my uncle sitting behind the sewing machine. He had his head down as if he was hiding. 'Come on, stop it now,' my gran said and put down the shopping bags.

'Tell her to stop it,' my aunty shouted and looked straight through my mum. 'She makes me sick.'

'I'd better move these then,' my mum said, pushing a bag of flour and packets of dried fruit to one side. 'I'm off now; I'm already late.'

My aunty moved to her right. 'You're not going till you tell me what you were up to,' she shouted.

'Nothing,' my mum said and lined up the packets of dried fruit. 'I keep telling you; nothing. What's wrong with you, are you deaf?'

'No, and I'm not daft either,' my aunty said. 'Why was the door locked then?'

'I've told you,' my mum sighed. 'It wasn't locked, it was stuck. How many more times. It always sticks in the winter, doesn't it.' She looked at my gran and so did I but my gran didn't say anything, so I did.

'Yes.'

'You've got to give it a kick,' my mum said.

'It's not the door that needs a kick,' my aunty said. 'And what about the curtains, were they stuck too?'

'I was washing my hair.' My mum pulled at her hair as if my aunty didn't know what hair looked like.

'That's right, she was,' I said. 'I saw her.'

'And I didn't want anybody to see in.'

'That's funny,' my aunty sort of laughed; 'since when have you been shy about anybody looking at you?'

'It depends who's looking,' my mum said and smiled at me.

'Anything in pants,' my aunty shouted, 'and especially if it's somebody else's husband.'

'Well that rules out Mike, doesn't it?' my mum said.

'What's that supposed to mean?' Aunty Enid asked.

'If you don't get it,' my mum said, 'never boil cabbage twice; I'm not interested in your Mike.'

My aunty looked at my uncle. 'Are you running out of men?' she asked. 'How many men do you need?' she began to shout.

'How many men have you got?' my mum said softly.

'You make me sick,' my aunty said and her mouth looked like a broken bottle. 'Sick!'

'I'll get the bucket for you.' My mum seemed to be enjoying it. 'Look, I'm going to be late.'

'You're not going anywhere,' my aunty said, moving to the corner of the table. 'I want to know.'

'What?' my mum said, looking at the clock.

'What you were doing with the door locked and the curtains closed.' My aunty was trembling.

'Having a seance,' my mum said. 'Trying to contact the dead. Nothing. Ask him.'

'You're a liar,' my aunty shouted and leaned across the table. 'I know you, you can't keep your hands off a man; there's something wrong with you.'

'But not him,' my mum interrupted.

'Don't blame him, I know you of old; you must have egged him on. I know what you're like.'

'Do you? What's that then?' my mum asked and cupped her ear.

'Like a bitch on heat but all the time. Everybody says so.'

For the first time my mum looked hurt; she looked at me as if she wanted me to say something. 'It takes two to tango,' my mum said, still looking at me.

'You're not all there,' my aunty said. 'Do you know that? That must be it. Did you drop her on her head when she was a baby?' My aunty looked at my gran.

'Stop it now,' my gran said.

'If she did,' my mum looked straight at my aunt, 'at least it would have been an accident; she'd have dropped you on purpose.'

'Mad filthy whore,' my aunty shouted. 'That's what you are.'

'Well it's nice to know I'm useful to somebody,' my mum said and smiled, but it wasn't one of her best smiles.

'You make me sick,' my aunty said.

'Here we go again,' my mum said and perked up a bit. 'Come here and let me put my fist down your throat.'

'You shouldn't be allowed to live with decent people,' my aunty said and stuck out her chin. 'Everybody knows about you and what you do. If you had any decency you'd go away and leave everybody in peace.'

'I know how much you would miss me if I did,' my mum said. 'I mean you wouldn't have anybody to talk about, would you.'

'Miss you?' my aunty said. 'I wouldn't miss you, I don't know anybody who would.'

'There's a few,' my mum said, 'no more than a few.'

'Nobody decent, I'll bet,' my aunty sneered and the colour rose up in her face.

'As the song says, "a decent man is hard to find",' my mum said. 'Isn't that right, Mum?'

'Decent. You don't know the meaning of the word.' My aunty was making herself angry again.

'I know this,' my mum said, looking at the clock. 'People should mind their own business; I don't talk about anybody.'

'Because you can't, that's why,' my aunty shouted.

'Because it's not important, that's why,' my mum shouted back; 'and it's none of my business what other people do. I'm not interested and you and nobody else can tell me what to do, so keep your beak out or I'll snap it off.'

'I'm warning you,' my aunty said, pointing her finger at my mum. 'Don't you so much as look at him again, do you hear?'

'The whole street can hear you,' my gran said.

'Well I mean it; don't go anywhere near him.' Then my aunty Enid gipped. At first I thought she was going to be sick but she started crying instead.

My uncle stood up and put his arm around her. 'Come on,' he said, 'let's go upstairs.'

They walked slowly towards the door. I looked at my mum; I knew she always wanted to have the last word and I wanted to stop her. Then she did it. She pursed her lips and squeaked as if she was calling a dog. My aunty Enid turned and lunged at my mum, but my mum picked up the bag of flour and threw it: it hit her smack in the face. The bag burst and covered her from head to foot in flour. The impact and the shock knocked her backwards. I knew my mum was a good shot but that was one of her best; even she looked surprised. My aunty turned and ran upstairs sobbing.

'You little bitch,' my uncle said and grabbed at my mum but missed. He began to chase her around the table.

'Stop it,' I shouted, 'leave her alone.' Then my mum slipped and fell against the sewing machine. My uncle pulled her up by the hair and began to shake her.

'You bloody bitch,' he shouted in her face. 'I've a good mind to throttle you.'

'Leave her alone,' I shouted and tried to pull him off her. 'Leave her alone. Leave her alone, let go of her.'

I ran over to the sink and grabbed the bread knife from the draining board and got in between them.

'Leave her alone or I'll kill you,' I screamed. 'Leave her; I'll kill you, I'll kill you, I'll kill you, I'll kill you.'

My uncle looked down at the knife and let go. I held up the knife at his throat. 'I'll kill you if you touch her; I'll kill you, I will.'

The words sounded as if they were coming from the cellar; my uncle took another step back.

'Mad,' he said, 'the pair of you,' and walked out of the kitchen shaking his head. 'Mad.'

I couldn't move; I just stood with the knife held out. 'Give it to me,' I heard my gran say, but I couldn't let go.

'Let go of the knife,' my mum said from behind, but I couldn't open my hand. A noise like an express train was going through my head and when it had passed I began to cry and dropped the knife.

My uncle Mike and aunty Enid went home and my mum didn't come back until the new year.

My birthday: I was thirteen.

The postman always came late on Saturday. I sat up in bed and listened. I could hear my grandad chopping firewood in the cellar; it was cold and I got back down into bed again. The smell of frying bacon got me up and I rushed downstairs, just as my birthday cards were pushed through the letterbox.

'Twenty-four,' I said as I opened the kitchen door. 'Look, Grandad, twenty-four cards.'

He put down the *Sporting Chronicle*. 'Twenty-five,' he said, sliding another envelope across the table. 'From your gran and me.'

I opened it and took out the money. 'Thanks,' I said and started two piles; one for the cards and one for the money.

'Go up and say thank you to your gran,' he said from behind his newspaper. 'You can take her a cup of tea.'

'I will, I will, in a minute,' I said and tore open another envelope.

'She'll like that, she's had a bad night; she's not well.'

'Nearly everybody's sent me money,' I said. 'Look, Grandad.'

He looked at the pile of money. 'I've got just the horse for you,' he said and laughed. 'Do you know what it's called? Birthday Boy.'

'Are you going to back it?' I asked and started to count my money again.

'Let's have a look,' he said and shook the paper to make the pages straight. 'Well, it's not done much,' he said slowly and turned to the back page, 'but it's come a fair distance; the trainer wouldn't have brought it all that way.' He turned back to the front page: 'No, that's the only one he's got, so he must think it's coming into form; I think I'll risk it each way.'

I made a neat pile with my money. I had enough.

'What about your mum; has she sent you a card?'

I pretended to check the cards, but I knew she hadn't. 'Maybe something will come in the second post,' I said, but I knew there wasn't a second post on Saturday.

After breakfast I caught the bus into town.

'Now, you're sure you're eighteen?' Hooky Barron said, taking the air rifle out of the shop window.

'Of course I am,' I said. He held the rifle close to his chest and looked at me. I got out the money and put it on the glass counter.

'Well, if you say so,' he said, loading it. 'If you say so . . .' He aimed and fired into a pile of newspapers: 'This'll stop a rhino,' he said and passed the rifle over to me. 'It's practical new,' he said, getting down behind the counter. 'I've got the box somewhere; here it is.' He held it up. '.22 Webley; it's a beauty, isn't it?'

I nodded and stroked the blue-black barrel.

'It's the best I've had in for a long time; go on, try it.'

I lifted it up and rested my cheek on the butt; I could still smell the varnish.

'Nice, eh?'

I had to cough to clear my throat. 'Yes.' I checked the

price on the label hanging from the trigger guard. 'I'll take it,' I said, handing it back.

'You won't be sorry,' he said and slid it back into its box.

I was beginning to get bored with my air rifle. I was fed up just shooting at cardboard targets, tin cans and pennies. The cat from across the road used to come and sit on the wall; I lined it up in my sights right between the eyes, but it just stared back as if it was daring me to break my promise.

One night, it was starting to get dark when I heard somebody tapping on the kitchen window. When I pulled back the curtains, Agar was standing there.

'Come outside,' he said, 'I've got something to show you.'

'What have you got?' I said when I got outside.

'Watch this,' he said, pulling out his air rifle from under his parka. He looked around for something to shoot at, then he took aim. When the pellet hit the dustbin, the pellet exploded; orange and white sparks flew off in all directions. I tried to grab his rifle. 'Get off,' he said, and pulled away.

'Do it again,' I said. This time he fired at the wall, the pellet ricocheted and sent a line of sparks spiralling over the wall.

'Where did you get them?' I knew now it was the pellets.

'I made them,' he said, hiding the rifle under his parka.

'How?' I ran to the gate to stop him getting away.

'It's easy,' he said, looking around for another way out, 'dead easy.'

'Tell me then.' I shut the gate.

'You won't tell anybody, will you?' he said.

'No I won't.'

'Well,' he said and made a long whistling sound.

'Come on,' I said. 'I won't tell.'

'You get some matches,' he said. Then he stopped.

'Yeah; then what?'

'You shave off the red bit . . .'

'And?'

'You fill up the pellet with it; that's all.'

'Is that it?' I said, moving away from the gate. 'How do you stop it coming out?'

'Oh yeah,' he said, turning back. 'You use a bit of silver paper; you pack it in tight, use the match to push it in. I tried plasticine at first, then some candle wax, but silver paper's best.'

I couldn't wait to try it. I made six in the kitchen and took them up to my bedroom. I lay on my bed with the window wide open and looked out across the roof tops like a sniper. The enemy were drain pipes, chimneys and television aerials. One aerial in the shape of an 'X' had a bull's eye at the centre and was just asking to be shot at. It was the one target I came back to night after night.

I kept my rifle under my bed, and if I woke up in the middle of the night I would always take my rifle and lean on the window sill; any suspicious-looking shadows were dropped with a single shot.

Summer came early, and the Lido opened one month earlier than normal. I was one of the first in and spread out my towel in my usual corner by the diving boards. After ten goes at a forward somersault dive, I lay on my towel and let the sun dry me.

'Hey, hey,' I heard somebody say, but I was half-asleep

and couldn't be bothered to open my eyes. 'Hey you, wakey-wakey.' I heard a man's voice say; then somebody kicked my foot. I opened my eyes. One of the swimming pool attendants was standing over me, an old man, tall and scrawny. He had a head like a tortoise and wore thick-lensed glasses; he worked in the changing room.

'What's that in aid of?' he said and pointed.

I looked down: I had an erection and my penis was sticking out of my swimming trunks, flat against my stomach. I pushed it to one side and back into my trunks. Two girls were pretending to read, but they were both giggling.

'Come on,' he said, 'you'd better get out.' I didn't move. 'Do you hear me? Changing room.' I got up. 'And wrap your towel around if you can't control yourself,' he said, turning to go. I didn't need the towel; I was soft now.

Keeping just one step behind his wooden clogs, I followed him back to the changing room.

'I want to have a word with you before you go,' he said, handing me my basket of clothes.

I was sneaking past his room when he came out: 'And where do you think you're . . .' He reached over and held my arm. 'Come in here.'

The small room was full of steam, a kettle stood on a single gas ring in the corner, and hundreds of bathing costumes hung on lines like washing.

'Now then,' he said, sitting down at a small desk. 'What's your name?'

I looked at the finger marks on my arm.

'Come on; you'd better tell me now before the police come.'

'Police?' I said and looked at the door.

'Don't bother,' he said, 'it's locked.'

The smell of chlorine was making my eyes water.

'Come on,' he snapped. 'You'll only make it worse for yourself; what's your name?'

'Stuart Broadly,' I said.

'Stuart Broadly,' he repeated, and slowly wrote it down. 'And where do you live, Stuart?'

'Eighty-seven, Ethel Road.'

'Oh yes, I know,' he said, and wrote it down.

'This is a very serious matter,' he said, putting down his pencil and swivelling around to face me. 'Isn't it?'

'Yes,' I agreed.

'Come here. Stand closer. I can't hear you.'

'Yes,' I said again, but louder, and shuffled forward.

'I think you're a wrong 'un, aren't you?'

'No,' I said.

'Well, I think you are . . . Has this happened before?'

'No, never,' I said and shook my head. 'It's the first time.'

He moved to the edge of the chair. 'Well, if it is the first time, I suppose I could put the police off . . . They trust me, you see; I often help them.'

'Honest,' I said hopefully. 'It's never happened before.'

'You wouldn't lie to me?' he said and narrowed his eyes. I continued to shake my head. 'I bet you touch yourself there when you're in bed,' he said. 'And what about when you're with your mates; do you touch each other then?'

'No,' I said. 'Never.'

'I know what young boys are like,' he said, sitting back in his chair. 'Well, perhaps I believe you, perhaps I don't,' he said, tapping his knee with a ruler.

'I'm telling you the truth, honest I am,' I said.

'What about now?' He moved forward again. 'Has it gone down?'

34

'Yes.' I looked down at my jeans. 'It's all right now.'

'But how do I know? I'll have to check first. I mean . . . I can't let you walk around like that, can I? You'll have to show me. Come on. I haven't got all day.'

I unzipped my jeans and pulled them down to my knees; then I pulled down my underpants and just stood there.

He stared for a long time; then he said: 'It still looks big to me.'

'It's not,' I said.

'You've still got a hard-on,' he said.

'No I haven't, it's . . .'

'I'll have to measure it.' He leaned forward and prodded me with his ruler. 'Go on,' he said. 'Put it on there. Nearly three inches,' he said. 'Well, that's big, isn't it? Very big,' and he slowly lifted the ruler up and down as if he was trying to guess the weight of it.

The kettle began to whistle but the steam blew the top off. He didn't seem to notice; he just stared and lifted the ruler up and down, up and down. Somebody started knocking on the door but he didn't seem to hear.

'There's somebody at the door,' I said, expecting it to be the police. They knocked again louder. He made a sound in his throat like a cat makes when you try to take its food away. He got up and opened the door and I pulled up my jeans.

'Mister –' (it wasn't the police) – 'my brother's cut his foot,' a young boy said. 'And we can't stop it bleeding.'

I ran straight through the gap between the old man and the boy.

'It's no good running,' he shouted after me. 'I know you now; the police will be coming to get you.'

I vaulted the turnstile and didn't stop until I got into my bedroom. They have a description of me, I thought. When they go to Stuart's they'll see it isn't him and somebody's sure to tell. I need to get away. If I was older I could emigrate to Australia; they'd never find me there. I got under the bed with my rifle and waited for the police. When I woke up it was dark. I went downstairs to the kitchen; my gran was boiling some milk.

'Where've you been?' she said, catching the milk just before it boiled over.

'Upstairs in bed,' I said.

'Not when your grandad looked, you weren't,' she said, and poured the boiling milk into a mug.

'I was underneath,' I said. 'What time is it?' I looked at the clock. 'I've got a headache,' and I held my forehead to make it look more convincing.

'Everybody's been looking for you.'

'Who?' I said, spinning round.

'Your grandad went down to the swimming pool, and Agar.'

'Anybody else?' I said.

'That funny little one . . .'

'Who?'

'The one you say smells.'

'Broadly?' I said. I felt sick.

'Yes,' she said, taking a biscuit out of the box. 'Three or four times. Are you hungry?'

'No.'

'Do you want an aspirin?'

'No, I'm going back to bed.'

I didn't get undressed, I lay on my bed with my rifle and listened. I didn't sleep much and when I did I dreamt about prison and my trial.

I'm standing at the bottom of an empty swimming pool. The swimming pool attendant is sitting on the high diving board dressed like a judge:

'You are charged with having an erection.'

'No.'

'An erection in a public place.'

'No.'

'How do you plead?'

'Not guilty.'

'But we have witnesses.'

All my friends are sitting around the pool and they begin to chant, 'Guilty, guilty, guilty.'

'Silence in court.' The judge taps the edge of the diving board with a ruler. 'Silence in court. This is a very serious offence; who said you could have an erection?'

'Nobody.'

'So, you admit you had one then? You can't have an erection without getting permission first.'

'Permission?'

'Yes, permission. You must complete forms, take tests, pass exams, get a licence, and anybody found in possession of an erection without a licence, in a *public place* . . .'

'Guilty, guilty,' my friends began chanting again.

'Silence. Now, before I pass sentence, you must drop your trousers.'

I pulled them down.

'Guilty, guilty, guilty.'

'I can't help it.'

'Silence. You have been found guilty and the sentence of this court is . . .' The judge lifts an enormous axe above his head . . .

It was light when I heard the bedroom door being opened.

I didn't turn over to see who was coming in; there was no way I could escape now. I should have left the window open and with a rope, but now it was too late; they were here. I knew before I turned over that there would be at least two policemen. I slowly turned around ... It was my mum ... in a new fur coat too. She was holding a tray with my breakfast on it.

'Are you better?' she said and sat on the edge of the bed.

'Mmm. A bit.'

'Are you hungry?' she asked, looking at my bacon sandwich and my mug of coffee.

'Yes,' I said and sat up.

My mum went over to the window.

'It's going to be hot,' she said opening the window, but she kept her fur coat on.

'Mum,' I said, taking the bacon out of the sandwich and leaving the bread. 'Have you ever thought about living in Australia?'

'Not very often, no.' She turned to look at me. 'Why, have you?'

'Yes,' I said casually. 'I wouldn't mind.'

'I thought you wanted to go to America.'

'Or America,' I said. 'I don't mind. Anywhere.'

'I'll think about it,' she said. 'Look at that sky ... Are you going swimming today?'

'No,' I said. 'I don't feel like it.'

'Go on, I'll pay.' She came over and stood by my bed. 'And ... I've got something for you, a bit late, but ...' She took some money from her bag, put it on the bed and walked to the door.

'Mum,' I said, just as she was about to close the door. She waited. 'Mum,' I said again.

'Well?' she said, waiting. 'Spit it out and read it.'

'You know when you get a hard-on . . .'

She froze. 'Sort of,' she said eventually, and came back into the room and sat on my bed.

'Well,' I said. It felt easier now I had started. 'There's this friend in my class at school and he's got himself into a bit of trouble.'

'With a hard-on?' my mum said, looking straight through me.

'Yes.'

'What's he done?' And she laughed.

'It's not funny, Mum; the police are after him. He could go to prison, couldn't he?'

'Depends what's he's been doing with it,' she said, widening her eyes.

'No, nothing. I . . . I mean he just had a hard-on.'

She stood up.

'You can't go to prison for that,' she said, 'although I sometimes think it wouldn't be a bad idea.'

'But what if somebody saw it?'

'Saw it?' my mum repeated. 'Saw it where?'

'Let's say – at the swimming pool,' I said.

My mum stared at me for a long time; then she sat down on the bed again and said: 'Tell me everything that happened to your friend. I'll just look out of the window and listen.'

When I had finished telling her she stood up and looked at me. She was angry; at first I thought she was going to hit me but she grabbed hold of my arms and dragged me downstairs. My gran came out to see what was going on.

'What are you doing?' my gran asked.

'It's a game,' my mum said, pulling me along the hallway.

'I've got a game you can play,' my gran said. 'It's called hoovering.'

When we got out into the street I stopped struggling.

'Where are we going?' I said.

'To the Lido,' my mum said, and I stopped walking but she gripped my arm tighter. 'You'll have to pull your arm off before you get away.' And she meant it.

When we got to the Lido there were twenty people waiting to go in. Mum pushed her way to the front, pulling me with her; we squeezed through the turnstile.

'You need a ticket,' the woman in the ticket office shouted and ran to the side door just as we turned the corner. 'Excuse me, you need a ticket to get in,' and stood in front of us. My mum pushed her against the wall.

'I'm going to get the manager,' the ticket woman shouted.

'You get the manager,' my mum shouted back. 'We'll be in the men's changing room.'

The old man was sitting behind the counter reading a newspaper. He held out his hand: 'Ticket,' he said, still reading his newspaper.

'Is this him?' my mum asked, pointing at him.

'Yes,' I said.

He stood up, and knocked over his stool.

'I want to have a word with you,' my mum said and lifted the counter leaf. He backed away.

'In there,' she pointed at the open door and followed him in, slamming the door shut.

It was like deep mid-winter in the changing room. Everybody froze, new arrivals were overcome by the silence, and their cries of 'what's up' trailed away.

When my mother came out the old man followed and stood in the open doorway. My mother was small and he seemed so big; it would have been so easy for him to knock her down with one swipe, but he just stood there with his head down.

'Now what's all this about?' the manager said, starting a thaw in the changing room.

My mother took him by the arm and led him over to an empty cubicle. I couldn't hear what she was saying, but she kept looking back at me and pointing at the old man. She was jabbing the manager in the chest and then she left him as if he'd been stabbed, leaning against the white tiled wall.

She walked quickly over to me. 'Right, that's settled. Let's go,' she said.

As we came to the corner of the counter, my mother stopped and looked at the old man. 'And you remember what I told you,' she said to him. He didn't lift his head but he looked at her and she leant across the counter and said slowly: 'If you so much as look at my boy again, I'll cut your balls off.' She took a broken ruler out of her pocket and threw the pieces at him. 'Do you hear me?'

'Yes,' the old man said and nodded his head.

'Leave the kids alone,' my mum said. 'Right?' The old man nodded. 'Because if you don't I'll speak to somebody about you and it won't be your balls they'll cut.'

My mum didn't speak until we turned into our street. 'Don't let people push you around,' she said suddenly. 'Don't be afraid to ask *why*, and to say *no*. You know, just because they're grown-ups and wearing a tie, it doesn't mean they're right.'

Instead of coming into the house with me, she walked past. 'I'm going into town,' she said. 'Won't be long.' And she smiled one of her great smiles, winked, and made a fist and shook it.

When I got into the house, there was a big man, a stranger, talking to my gran. 'This man is a policeman,' my grandmother said to me.

'Hello,' he said standing up. 'Have you got an air rifle?'

Another letter. I turned it over: S.W.A.L.K. written across the flap. I opened it and read:

'I watch you every day come home from school. I love you.'

It was signed with a red lipstick kiss.

Joan Taylor's parents always went out on Friday night. She was the first girl I kissed who put her tongue into my mouth. When she did it the first time, I told her off.

'Don't,' I said, pulling my head back as if I'd had an electric shock.

'Don't you like it?' she said.

'No.' And I sat on the edge of the sofa.

'Do you like this then?' She sat up behind me. 'I read about this in a book,' she said and started kissing my ears. 'What about this?' she whispered and poked the tip of her tongue in my ear.

'No, that's it,' I said, pushing her away and standing up. 'Look, I'd better be off, I've got to get up early tomorrow; I'm helping Mr Philips do his milk round.'

'Give me one kiss before you go,' she said, sliding back on to the sofa.

I went to kiss her, then stopped. 'You won't do it again, will you?' I said. 'Only proper kissing?' I put my hand on her breast but she pushed it away. At first I thought she was just stopping me; then she put my hand back but this time I was touching skin.

'My mum goes mad,' she explained, 'when I get dirty marks on my blouse.' She moved my hand over. 'The other one feels left out.'

Breathing was not easy.

'Do you want to know something?' she said, unhooking the front of her bra. I prayed to God to let me live for just another five more minutes.

'I was the first girl in my class to have a pyramid.'

'Were you?' I said. 'A pyramid? What's a . . . ?'

At the sound of a car braking she gripped my hand. 'Christ,' she said, sitting up. 'They're early.' I left by the back door.

The light was on in my mum's bedroom; she was back. 'Boo,' she said, looking up from painting her toe-nails. She had a Val-Pak on; her face was all white except for her eyes and mouth.

'I knew you were back,' I said, closing the door behind me.

'You just caught me,' she said, starting on the other foot.

'Why, what were you doing?' I said.

She looked up but didn't say anything. I sat next to her on the bed.

'Don't jog me,' she said, digging me with her elbow. 'I've got to get this right first time.' She held her breath and concentrated on her little toe. 'Do you know what the time is?' she said, letting it out.

'Yes,' I said, looking at my watch then staring up at the ceiling.

'Well, come on then, you dozy sod, don't play your silly games with me; what is it?'

'Five and twenty to ten.'

'Five and twenty to ten,' she repeated and laughed. 'You sound like your grandad.'

She walked to the wash basin on her heels and rinsed her face. 'I'm late at usual . . . Which one?' She held up two dresses.

'That one,' I said, pointing at the nearest.

'Oh, don't say that, I haven't got any shoes to go with it.'

'The other one then,' I said.

'Are you sure?'

'They're both nice,' I said, going to the window and watching the long grey Jag trying to park. When I turned round she was dressed and spraying perfume everywhere.

'Where are you going?' I said, trying on her fur coat, but she was drawing a fine line from the corner of her eye and I couldn't understand what she said. 'Where are you going?' I growled and stood behind her.

'Night school,' she said, turning round and pulling the fur coat off me. 'Come on, help me on with this,' she said, handing me the coat.

'Will you come to school next week?' I said as she admired herself in the mirror. The Jag sounded its horn.

'I might.' She turned to the left. 'Depends,' and then to the right, 'why?'

'I've won a prize.'

'Did you?' She got up close to the mirror. 'What for? Shooting?'

'Art,' I said. 'I've won first prize. I made a sculpture out of tin cans, two men fishing.' She was nearly ready to go. 'One holding the net and the other man taking the fish out.' She was looking for her handbag. 'All in tin.' She opened a drawer and took out a pair of gloves.

'Is it cold?' she said, trying them on.

'No,' I said.

'Well, I don't need these then,' she said, putting the gloves back.

'Mr Andrews says he's going to put it in for another competition.' The car tooted again. 'You will come, won't you?' She pulled up the collar of her coat. 'You will, won't you?'

'All right, I promise; if I can, I will,' she said. 'How do I look?'

'OK,' I said, giving in.

'OK? Is that all? Look again,' she said, and held me at arm's length.

'You look terrific,' I said. 'You know you do.'

'I know,' she said and winked at me, 'but it's nice to be told.'

The car tooted again but this time longer.

'Hello,' she said pulling me closer, 'what's this?' She touched my neck and showed me the lipstick on her fingertips. 'Lipstick?' she said, trying to touch my neck again, but I pulled away. 'Don't tell me you've started already,' she said, following me to the mirror.

'Started what?' I said, rubbing the red smudges off my neck and turning up my collar.

'You know,' she said, trying to get round in front of me. The car tooted. 'He'll wait,' she said, glancing at the window. 'Let me have a look at you,' she said, holding my shoulders and turning me round. 'I never noticed,' she said eventually, pulling the points of my collar down. 'I don't know where to start,' and she gave a short laugh. 'I don't want you getting yourself into any sort of trouble,' she said. 'Do you know what I mean? Girl trouble.'

'Yes,' I said.

She gave another short laugh. 'Are you just kissing or is it more serious?'

'No,' I said.

'No, it is more serious, or no, just kissing?' she said. 'Because if it is . . . Who are you going out with?'

'Joan Taylor,' I said.

'Joan Taylor?' she repeated slowly. 'Bab's girl? The wool shop?'

'Yes.'

'But she's too old for you.'

'She's only two years older than me,' I protested.

'Two years,' my mum said and paused to think about it. 'She's like a woman, full grown . . . you're just a kid.'

'I'm not,' I had to disagree.

'You are, never mind about your muscles; Mr Universe or not, you're still just a kid.'

The car tooted a long blast but my mum didn't seem to hear it.

'Have you . . .' she started, 'done anything?'

'No,' I said. I could feel my face getting redder.

'Kissing?' my mum said. 'Only kissing; is that all?'

'Yes,' I said.

'You've not been playing Mums and Dads, have you?'

'What's that?' I said.

'Or doctors and nurses?'

'Doctors and nurses?' I said. 'No, we just listen to records.'

'With the light out?' My mum let go of me. 'On the rug in front of the fire? Yes? Very romantic, very dangerous.'

'No,' I said, determined never to see Joan again.

'But you will,' my mum said, making a final check in the mirror. 'You will, sooner or later, you will.' I shook my head. 'You will,' she said, 'and it's no good you saying you won't,' and she pointed her finger at me, 'so don't make silly promises that you're not going to keep, and it's no good me saying don't do it because if it was that easy . . .'

The car tooted three short blasts.

'I've got to go now,' she said, then stopped and opened her handbag. 'I don't know,' she said, staring into her handbag. 'I don't know . . .' Then she took out an oblong packet and handed it to me. I turned it around and read: *three Durex*.

'Do you know what they are?' she asked.

'Yes,' I said, staring at the packet and starting to blush.

'So, you know how to use them.'

I said I did. My face was getting redder.

'I mean, do you know,' she laughed, 'how to put one on?'

'Yes,' I said, feeling sunburnt all over.

'So, you don't want me to show you then?' she said and laughed again.

I just wanted her to go and kept staring at the packet.

'Be careful,' she said. 'Be careful.'

I didn't look up until she had closed the door and I heard her going down the stairs.

When my gran came out of hospital, the back room on the ground floor was made into a bedsitting room.

'You'll have to look after yourself now,' she said, squeezing the border of the counterpane with each short breath.

'I already do a lot more than any of my friends,' I said, putting a mug of Bengers on her bedside table.

'I know you do, you're a good boy. I don't know what we'd do without you.' I enjoyed our talks late at night in her pink bedroom. 'You can't expect your grandad to cook and, as for the washing machine and ironing, well, he's just like a baby. He's never had to do it. I've done every-thing for him.' She began to cough. 'I even bought his shirts for him.' She started coughing again.

'Do you want your medicine?' I said, picking up the bottle and shaking it.

'No,' she said, wiping her mouth with her handker-chief, 'it's not time.' I fluffed up her pillows the way I'd seen the nurses in hospital do. 'Your aunty Enid will come in on Mondays, so that'll be a big help.'

'I haven't got time to do your bed this week,' my aunty Enid said as soon as I walked into the kitchen. 'You'll have to shake 'em and turn 'em,' she said, taking her cup and saucer over to the sink. 'When I've done the windows, I'm off.'

I looked in to see my gran but she was sleeping. So I went up to my bedroom and changed into my shorts. I had to do three by ten sets of squats with the bar bells, but I started with my favourite exercise – chinning the bar. I had found an old towel rail in the cellar and screwed it to the beam that ran across the ceiling. I could do more than anybody and was nearly able to do it with just one hand.

'It can't be done,' John Alan had sneered when he saw me training in the school gym.

'It's a bet,' I said, and when I went back to school in September, John Alan's big mouth cost him his American Bristol fibreglass fishing rod.

I was doing perfect 'chins' (arms full stretch and straight legs), when my aunty came into my bedroom. She was holding a yellow duster in one hand and a bottle of Windowlene in the other.

49

'This lot must have cost a fortune,' she said, trying to pull a pair of chest-expanders.

'Only five pounds,' I said, dropping from the bar and showing her how to do it. 'Saint Luke's jumble sale, not bad hey? Five pounds for everything.'

'It looks like a lot of hard work,' she said, staring at the pictures of body-builders on the bedroom wall. 'They look so oily, and look at that one, he's like a gorilla.'

'Look at this,' I said, flexing my lateral spread.

'Don't get too big,' she said.

'What's too big?' And I turned to show her my back.

'You know,' she said, taking a chair over to the window, 'out of proportion.'

'What do you think?' I said, flexing my biceps.

'I think I'd better do these windows or I'll be late.' She held the back of the chair. 'But I think I've run out of steam.'

'I'll do it,' I said.

'I should wash these,' she said, pulling back the curtains. 'I'll do them next week.'

I folded the duster to find a clean place.

'You have a handsome body,' she said quietly, almost as though she was thinking aloud, and she began to stroke the back of my leg. 'Handsome . . . I'll see you next week.' She turned to go.

'What's this,' she said, bending down and picking something up. I didn't take much notice. I was just starting to do some curls with the bar bells, when she turned around and I saw her face. I put them down again. 'What's this?' she said, coming over to me with the packet of Durex in her hand.

'I don't know,' I said, feeling the floor ripple. I felt as if everything in the room was about to explode.

'You don't?' she said. 'Well, I do,' looking back at the door, then at me.

'I've no idea,' I said, turning my head and pretending to read the packet. 'They're not mine.' Lies raced through my head: 'Perhaps a dog brought them in,' I tried.

'A dog?' my aunty said. 'What dog? We haven't got a dog.'

'It could have been Kim,' I said, 'across the road. He could have brought them in.'

'Up here? That dog's so scared of your grandad, it doesn't even look at this house.'

'Well, how do I know then,' I said, trying to think of somebody to blame. 'I have no idea.'

'No? I'll bet you haven't,' she said, looking inside the packet, '. . . and there's one missing.'

'Well it's got nothing to do with me,' I said.

'I can see you've got a lot of your mother in you,' she said and waited for me to answer. Perhaps I could say I found them in the street, I thought.

'Well?' she said again.

'Well, what?' I said.

'If this is the result of all your body-building, I'll get your grandad to throw this lot out.'

'I keep telling you . . .' I said.

'And I thought you were such a good boy, Granny's little pet. She's forever going on about what a little angel you are and so clever,' she said, taking hold of my arm. 'Let's see what your gran's got to say now.'

When she opened the bedroom door my mum was leaning against the door frame.

'Where are you going?' my mum asked, making my aunty step backwards into the bedroom, 'and why all the shouting?'

'This,' my aunty said, holding the packet of Durex up to her face. My mother laughed.

'That's typical, that is,' my aunty said, 'and you think it's funny ... I've just ...'

'I know,' my mum said, 'I was listening and now you want to go down and upset Mum.'

'She should know,' my aunty said.

'Know what?' my mum said, pushing the packet of Durex away.

'This,' my aunty said, thrusting the packet of Durex into my mother's face again, 'and there's one missing.'

My mum took the packet from my aunt. 'So what,' she said, looking inside. 'I think it's a good idea. I'm always telling everybody what a clever son I've got.' She gave me a quick smile.

'Clever?' my aunty said.

'Yeah,' my mum said, putting her back against the door. 'Clever. That's why I gave them to him.' She put her finger up to her lips. 'Shh ... Mum's having a nap.'

'You gave ...' my aunty said and looked at me, her mouth open, '... them ... to him. What for?'

'What for?' my mum said, pushing herself off the door and going face to face with my aunty.

'But he's only a kid,' my aunty said, moving away.

'He's not a kid,' my mum said. 'He's a young man, he's growing up. Kids don't stay kids for long these days; so I had a little talk with him about the birds and the bees.' My aunty stared at my mum. 'The facts of life,' my mum said, shrugging her shoulders. 'You know, S.E.X. You remember? Fucking.'

I had never heard any woman use that word before.

'What?' my aunty said, her face flushing crimson.

'I thought it was about time he knew,' my mum said. 'Well, he already knew, a bit, didn't you? I mean where everything went, or wanted to go. I just wanted to make sure it was safe.'

'And I thought Joan Taylor was a nice girl,' my aunty said, looking at me sideways.

'Nice but stupid,' my mum said. 'She would be a nice girl if she got pregnant. Is that what you mean?'

The earthquake was over. The floor stopped moving.

'No, I don't mean that,' my aunty said. 'They shouldn't be doing it and you shouldn't be encouraging him.'

'Don't be ridiculous,' my mum said, spitting out the words. 'They don't need any encouragement.'

'They shouldn't be doing it,' my aunty tried again.

'Well, I think you should be pleased,' my mum said. 'I mean, it seems so sensible, I mean, responsible.'

'It's disgusting; you're disg – '

'Well, I'm proud of him. I wish somebody had explained it all to me when I was his age; perhaps I could have made something of myself –'

'Instead of . . . ?' My aunty interrupted.

'Instead of getting pregnant,' my mum said, conceding a point. 'Getting pregnant at seventeen closed a lot of doors for me.'

'You haven't done so badly for yourself,' my aunty said. 'You dress like a film star. You live here rent-free and you never do anything for it. I've never seen you wash so much as a cup and saucer and now it's me who's got to look after the house.'

'I'm a bit clumsy, you see,' my mum said. 'I break things, Mum says . . .'

'On purpose,' my aunty interrupted. 'I bet you break things on purpose.'

'Is that what you'd do?' my mum said. 'You always were devious.'

My aunty snatched the packet of Durex from my mum. 'And as for you, golden boy . . .' She looked at me again, trying to get past my mum.

'You know the trouble with you?' my mum said, holding the door knob.

'I don't want to hear any more,' my aunty said, covering her ears with her hands.

'No,' my mum said, pushing her back. 'No, you don't want to hear but I'm going to tell you anyway; this'll be good for you. Open wide. You're jealous.'

'Jealous?' my aunty laughed. 'Jealous of who?'

'Everybody,' my mum said. 'Jealous of him, jealous of Joan Taylor. And, only God knows why, jealous of me.'

My aunty tried to open the door but my mum wouldn't let her. 'Don't be mean,' my mum said gently. 'Don't tell Mum. She doesn't need all this, not now. You know how poorly she is; why make it worse.' Then my mum opened the door just a few inches for my aunty. 'I'm asking you. Please,' and she put her hand on her shoulder, 'don't tell her.'

'She ought to know,' my aunty said, pushing my mother's hand away.

'Do you remember when we were kids,' my mother started slowly, 'and I brought that little black pup home?'

'What?' My aunty sounded surprised.

'Prince,' my mum said. 'It followed me home from school. Do you remember?'

'What about it?' my aunty said and relaxed.

'But you do remember it, don't you?' my mum said.

'Yes, I remember it,' my aunty said. 'I remember Dad said none of us could have a dog, but he let you because you were the baby. You always got what you wanted.'

I could see in my aunty's face a pain that had had no time to heal.

'Well, I didn't get to keep it long, did I?' my mum said. 'Did I? Do you remember that too?'

'Yes,' my aunty remembered.

'About a month, that's all,' my mum said. 'And do you remember why?' My aunty didn't answer.

'It kept peeing everywhere, didn't it?'

'Yes,' my aunty said, nodding her head, 'I remember.'

'I never could understand it,' my mum said. 'I walked miles with it every night but every morning there would be another pool of pee. Dad warned me; just once more and he would get rid of it. I used to get up early every morning to see if it had done it so I could clean it up before anybody saw it, but it kept on doing it. So in the end I kept it in the back yard, but somehow it still managed to get in and do it. Well, one morning I got up and went to the kitchen window and it was still outside. I could see it; I can see it now sleeping in an old pram. So I started to go upstairs. Half-way up, I saw the front room door was open; I looked in and I saw you crouching down on the new carpet. I suppose I thought you were reading or something. I went back to bed, then we all got up at the usual time, had breakfast and went to school, but when I came back Prince was gone; he'd done an enormous pee on the new carpet.'

My aunty looked up at my mum and my mum stared back. 'But it wasn't Prince, was it? And all the other times too; it was you that was pissing everywhere. Funny, the things you remember years later.'

My mum opened the door for my aunty. We listened to her go downstairs, put on her coat and quietly close the front door.

My mother's laugh woke me up. I jumped out of bed and stood by the window to watch. The taxi driver was holding her hand; she was trying to pull away but he wouldn't let go. When he did, she nearly fell over. He drove off and she gave him the 'V' sign but she was laughing when she turned round.

After breakfast I went to her bedroom and quietly opened the door. The thick curtains were drawn. I crept in but I couldn't see a thing.

'I've got a gun,' my mother said slowly, 'bullets too.'

'Is that all?' I said. 'Can I open the curtains?'

'Can I open the curtains?' she repeated. 'Can you? I don't know if you can. How many guesses do I get? Have you broken your arms or something? You mean, may I open the curtains, don't you?'

I didn't answer; she was in one of her awkward moods.

'Go on then,' she said, 'let's see what sort of a day it is.' I pulled back the curtains. 'Same as yesterday,' she said, and turned over.

'You know the art competition,' I said, sitting on the bed. 'I told you about it.'

'What about it?' she said from under the quilt.

'I won a prize.'

'I know, you told me.'

'Well, there's an exhibition from the other schools, from all over, and mine; it's going to be in London.

57

Look.' I held out an invitation card. 'Look.'

My mother turned over and took it. '. . . 195 Piccadilly . . . May eleventh . . . eleven o'clock. That's very good,' she smiled and gave it back to me.

'That's next week,' I said. 'Will you come with me?' She didn't say anything. 'It says: "Admits two". Look.' I held out the card again.

'Doesn't your gran want to go?' she said, rubbing her face against the pillow.

'She's not well,' I said, reading the invitation for the millionth time. 'She might have to go to hospital.'

'Hospital?' my mum said, turning over again.

'Gran says you've got to come with me; you will, won't you?'

'Next Tuesday,' my mum said, sitting up.

'There's a train at seven o'clock to King's Cross. I've checked.'

'Tuesday,' she said to herself. 'No, I'll meet you there,' and she slid under the bedcovers. 'What was the number?' I looked at the invitation, but I already knew it.

'195 . . .'

'Piccadilly,' she finished for me.

'At eleven o'clock,' I said.

'I'll meet you there. All right?' she said. 'Outside, at eleven o'clock. Pass me my handbag, will you?'

My gran had already given me some money but I didn't tell my mum that. She gave me another five pounds.

'Now let me sleep,' she said and pulled the quilt over her head, 'and close the curtains before you go.'

I was just about to shut the door when my mum asked: 'Do you know how to get there? From King's Cross, I mean, to Piccadilly? You take the Piccadilly line, the blue one, to Piccadilly Circus – you don't have to change, it's straight through – then ask.'

I stood in the open doorway and looked back into the dark room.

'Good night,' my mum said in a silly voice.

'You won't forget, will you?' I said.

'No,' she said, turning over and looking at me.

'Promise,' I said.

'Yes,' she said.

'Go on then,' I said. 'Promise.'

'Promise.'

'If you don't . . .'

'*Good night,*' she shouted and I closed the door.

When I came back from school I went up to my mother's bedroom again but the door was locked. She locked it from the inside when she didn't want to talk to anybody. On Fridays I didn't stay for school dinners because I didn't like fish. I tried the bedroom door and it was open, but she had gone. Her wardrobe was locked, so she hadn't just gone out, she would be gone for a few days. I tried the drawers of the dressing table; they were locked too. Perhaps she would be gone for a week, maybe two. I hoped she wouldn't forget. Then I looked in the mirror. She had written across it in lipstick: 195 Piccadilly – Tuesday, 11 o'clock. I smiled.

I enjoyed reading the posters on the escalators: 'AMANI FOR HAIR' and 'PLAYTEX BRAS WITH CIRCULAR STITCH'. Then I saw a poster advertising the exhibition but with my sculpture on it. I turned around but I couldn't see it; I wanted to run back up the escalator to see it again but I couldn't, so I got off at the bottom and went back up the other escalator. Then I saw another. They were everywhere. Posters of my sculpture. I kept going up and down the escalators just to see them.

'I did that,' I said to a woman and pointed at the poster. I saw a man in uniform watching me. He looked as if he was waiting for me to come up again, so I went to catch the train.

When I got to the platform there was the poster again, but this time it covered the whole wall from floor to ceiling, my little fishermen were ten feet tall and so was I.

I waited for ages but she didn't come. Then I saw Mr Andrews, my art teacher, and his wife Madame (she was French) walking towards me.

I wasn't sure what to say. When they saw me they both smiled. Mr Andrews put his arm around me and shook my hand. 'Well done,' he kept saying.

'Your beautiful sculpture is everywhere,' Madame said and she kissed me on both cheeks. 'Have you seen?'

Mr Andrews was wearing a tweed suit with a waistcoat and bow tie; Madame was wearing a black cloak lined in orange. They looked so interesting and I was so pleased that they were my friends. I looked left and right again, then went in.

The photographers took photographs of me holding the sculpture and journalists asked me questions. I wanted her to come in now, to see me like this. I was sure she would come.

'Would you like to have tea with us?' Mr Andrews said. 'Where shall we go?'

'You choose,' Madame said.

'We could go to Fortnum and Mason,' Mr Andrews suggested, 'or how about the Royal Academy?'

I said I didn't mind, then said the Royal Academy. It

sounded best. After tea we caught a taxi to King's Cross and returned home together.

I could see the light was on in my gran's room; she was waiting up for me.

'. . . And it will be in all the papers tomorrow,' I said, holding my grandmother's hand. 'And then we all went for tea. You should have seen it, Gran; it was fantastic, really fantastic.'

'What did your mum say?'

'She thought it was fantastic too,' I lied, 'but she didn't stay long.'

'Well, anyway, you're a clever boy,' she said and squeezed my hand. 'I always knew you were clever; you've got it here,' and she tapped my forehead, 'and here,' she touched my hands. 'Show me,' she said and I held up my hands. 'Creative hands,' she said, 'they'll make you a fortune one day. I'm as pleased as Punch. We're so proud of you, you've made up for everything. Now off you go to bed; your grandad will get all the papers in the morning.'

Before I went to bed I went into my mother's bedroom and wiped the lipstick off the mirror. I picked up a lipstick. I wanted to write something, anything so long as it was nasty, but I couldn't think of anything to say.

Something woke me up. I listened . . . Nothing . . . There it was again, somebody calling my name. I got out of bed and looked down into the street . . . I could see somebody; it was nearly three o'clock, even Agar wasn't that crazy. Then I saw who it was: my mother.

I ran downstairs; I knew all the steps that creaked and missed them. When I opened the door she was sitting on the doorstep with her back towards me.

'I waited for you all day,' I said. 'Thank you very much.' She turned her head and looked up at me. Her face was covered in blood; both eyes looked like ripe plums, her lips were swollen and caked with dried blood.

'I'm sorry,' she whispered. I nearly fainted.

Slowly she stood up; her dress was ripped to shreds, her legs looked as if she'd been dragged across a building site. 'I'm sorry,' she said again. She tried to walk up the steps. 'I don't think I can make it,' she said, and crawled on her hands and knees into the house. I knelt down beside her and put her arm over my shoulder and slowly I got her to her feet. 'Don't let your gran see me like this,' she said. 'Help me up to my bedroom.'

'What happened?' I said when I sat her on the bed. 'Have you been in a car crash?'

'Yes, that's it, that's what happened,' she said, looking down at her arms and legs.

'You should go to hospital,' I said, closing the bedroom door.

'No, I can't,' she said. 'I'll be all right, go to the bathroom and get some Dettol.'

When I came back she was lying on the bed. 'You'll have to undress me,' she said and tried to smile; then I saw that one of her front teeth was missing. 'Bring those towels over here,' she said, pointing at the washbasin. I knew how to use Dettol. Miss Briggs at school always used it when somebody cut themself. 'You'll have to rip the dress,' my mum said, closing her eyes. She tried to use the towels to cover herself.

She was beaten everywhere: her back was covered with red cuts like half moons. I wiped the blood from her face; I think her nose was broken. I don't know how long it took me, but I cleaned every cut and bruise from head to foot. When I had finished I wrapped her in a bath towel, put my arms around her shoulders, and rested her head against a pillow. I switched out the light and stayed with her.

The birds were just beginning to sing. Tea at the Royal Academy, 195 Piccadilly, seemed a long time ago.

I didn't say goodbye to my gran when she went into hospital. I was angry, but I can't remember why. I stood in the bay of the window in the front room and watched her being lifted into the ambulance. You'll be back, I said under my breath, you'll be back. In the afternoon I went down to the park to see if anybody was around.

'You know St Joseph's?'

I knew it was Stuart before I turned round to see.

'No,' I said, walking away.

'I know how to get in,' he said, catching up with me. 'Look,' he said, taking a large ripe pear out of his pocket.

'What about the gardener, Limpit, and his dog?' I said, taking the pear and starting to eat it.

'He won't see us. I'll show you,' he said, taking another pear out of his pocket. 'Come on.'

We stopped walking when we saw a rat coming out of a grate. We waited until it was about six metres away then we ran at it. It made it back to the grate but I caught it by the tail with my foot and it hung down into the drain squeaking. I didn't want to touch it and I didn't want to let go. Eventually the tail broke off and the rat fell into the water below.

Stuart threw his half-eaten pear after it but had to force it through the bars by stamping on it.

'Where are we going?' I said, looking back at St Joseph's College.

'You know Three Ponds?' Stuart said.

I took the pin out of my handgrenade: 'One – two – three,' I counted and lobbed the core of my pear over a wall wiping out a nest of German machine gunners.

'Know it?'

'Of course I know it. I showed it to you, didn't I?'

'Well, you know the wall?'

I stopped to think about it. 'It's got glass on the top, like you,' I sneered and started walking again.

'Not all the way,' Stuart said, poking his tongue out just to let me know this was top secret. 'Well, that wall goes all the way round to St Joseph's, you don't even have to get down.'

'You'd better be right, Broadly . . .'

We had been crawling on our hands and knees along the top of the wall for about ten minutes when he turned around and grinned. 'Look,' he said and pointed with his head. 'What did I tell you?'

It was just starting to get dark and the yellow pears seemed to glow as if they had little candles inside them. St Joseph's College was a Roman Catholic School for girls. Some of them were boarders and from where I was sitting I could see right into the dormitories and showers. At first I couldn't believe my eyes. About six girls were in the showers. I nearly fell off the wall.

'Look,' I said with a dry throat, 'they're all nude.'

Stuart stopped picking pears for a few seconds and looked. 'Yeah,' he said, pushing a pear down inside his shirt, 'then they have prayers. They pray between lessons, they even pray when they go to the bog.'

'Can't you see?' They haven't got a stitch on,' I said but he wasn't interested.

'I'm not waiting all night for you; let me get

past,' Stuart said, looking to the side of me.

When we got to Three Ponds, we climbed down and ran.

'Did you see them?' I said, checking that I hadn't been dreaming.

'Do you know how much these cost in the shops?' Stuart said as we slowed down and started to walk. 'I know where I can sell these,' he said, holding up a pear. I hadn't taken any. 'I'll show you another way home,' he said, putting the pear back into his shirt. I didn't argue with him.

'I know this way,' I said as we climbed onto the flat roofs of a row of garages. 'This comes out into the builders' yard.'

We crouched down and ran, keeping below the skyline like commandos. Suddenly there was a crack and Stuart disappeared in front of me. I looked into the hole but couldn't see a thing. 'Stuart, Stuart,' I said, 'are you all right?'

'I'm all right,' he whispered back. 'I'm all right.' I could hear him moving around, then he switched on a light.

'Can you get out?' I said and looked around to see if anybody had seen us.

'I'll put all these boxes together; it's easy,' and he started moving them over. 'Look at this,' he said. 'Mars bars, Kit Kats, Bounty bars; it's all chocolates and sweets.' He sounded as if he was going to have a fit.

'They're Mr Marks's,' I said. 'The sweet shop.'

Stuart got rid of all his pears and started ripping open the boxes. 'Crunchies,' he said, 'my favourite. Come down.' I hesitated. 'It's dead easy to get out,' he said. I lowered myself in.

*

Stuart must have gone back because next day he'd brought loads of chocolate to school and was selling it. I kept mine under the bed. That afternoon I was late getting back to school so I took a chance and climbed over the wall and ran across the school car park. I looked and looked again when I saw Stuart sitting in the headmaster's room talking to a policeman.

I wanted to keep running but a teacher saw me and told me that if I didn't get a move on I'd be late. He held the door open for me. 'David, will you go to the headmaster's office?'

I was expecting it; still my stomach went like a slug when you put salt on it. I stood by the open office door; I could see Stuart sitting in a side room. When he saw me he stuck his tongue out.

'Come in, David,' the headmaster said, taking hold of my arm and leading me into his office. 'Sit down, sit down,' he said, pointing at the chair. 'We had a phone call about ten minutes ago . . . from your . . .' he looked at the pad 'your aunty . . . Edna?'

'Enid,' I said.

'Enid,' he repeated. 'I understand your grandmother's not well. Your uncle is coming to collect you.'

Just then my uncle's car came into the school car park.

'Are you listening to me?' he said, swivelling round in his chair to see what I was looking at. 'You can leave by the staff entrance,' he said, standing up.

As I got closer to the car I could see that my uncle was not alone; my grandad was with him and he was wearing a tie. As I got closer, my grandad got out of the car and I could see that his eyes were red.

The church was full. I stood next to my grandad in the front pew. There was a strong smell of old clothes and black Radium shoe dye.

'. . . and he will be greatly missed,' the vicar said with that silly voice that vicars use. I looked at him. 'A man who was kind to everybody.'

'It's a bit early, isn't it?' my grandad said, taking out his pocket watch.

'A man who spent his life helping others . . .' Now everybody was staring at the vicar.

'Sarah, Sarah?' The vicar coughed.

'I think the penny's just dropped,' my grandad said to everybody. I waited for my mum to laugh but she didn't. When we left the church I found out why she hadn't. She wasn't there.

I saw her getting out of a car and, realizing that she was too late, stand on the opposite side of the road. When all the cars had gone back to my gran's house, I was left alone with my mother. 'Never mind,' she said, 'we can walk back. Do you want some chewing gum?'

Since the car accident she hadn't had the same bouncy walk. It wasn't long ago that she could run as fast as me. Her nose was still a bit swollen and the bump never went down.

'What are you going to do about your tooth?' I said,

taking off my tie and rolling it up before putting it in my pocket.

'I thought I might get a gold one,' she said, showing me her teeth. 'What do you think?' And she pushed the tip of her tongue through the gap in case I couldn't see it.

'Terrible,' I said. 'I hate gold teeth. Why don't you get an ordinary one?'

'I fancy a gold one; it'll make me look foreign, exotic and "misteriosa": olé,' and she stopped and stamped her foot.

It didn't take much to get my mum going but just then a lorry-load of builders went by and whistled at her, and of course she whistled back.

'Mum, you've got a grey hair,' I said and went to pull it out.

'Leave it,' she said and covered the side of her head with her hand. 'Pull it out and five more will grow.'

When we arrived home everybody had gone. Grandad was in the kitchen trying to wash up. He was wearing one of my gran's aprons over his suit and he still had his cap on.

'You're here then,' he said, without turning round. Mum's usual reply was, 'no it's somebody else' but she was just starting on a ham sandwich so she didn't say it.

The kettle was boiling and Grandad took it off the gas.

'I'm just going to make a cup of tea,' he said. My mum stood by the door ready to make a quick getaway.

'I don't know,' he said, pouring the boiling water into the pot. He shook his head slowly. 'I don't know.' Mum quietly opened the door. 'Couldn't even be on time for your mother's funeral.' Mum didn't say a thing; she knew it would be best to let him get it off his chest, so she came back and sat down at the table. Grandad poured out the tea and put four sugars in for everybody.

'She didn't look bad,' he said, pouring his tea into a saucer. Mum pushed back her chair. 'Where are you going?' Grandad looked at her for the first time. She bit her bottom lip. 'Like a cat on hot bricks you are.'

Mum took a sip of tea; I knew she wouldn't like it with sugar. 'I've been thinking,' Grandad said, 'the best thing I can do, now that she's gone.' We both looked up. 'This house is too big,' he said, 'I can't manage this place; I'd be a fool to try. I can't expect David to do all the housework; he already does more than most.'

'I don't mind,' I said. 'I like doing things in the house.'

'And as for you,' Grandad said and looked at my mum. 'Well, you're worse than useless.'

'Thanks very much,' my mum said and pushed her chair back again.

'Enid says I should go and live with them. She says they'll do out the attic for me; you too.' He looked at me. 'You can come too if you want to . . . or do you want to stay with your mum?'

'You mean here?' I said and looked up at the ceiling as if I had X-ray eyes and could see right through the house.

'Your own place,' he said. 'I'll get shot of this lot.'

'So we're being thrown out,' my mum said, pushing the table forward and making the cups and saucers rattle. 'Is that it?' And she stood up.

'I always thought you wanted your own place,' Grandad said.

'No, I didn't, never, I like it here.' She walked over to the kitchen window and stared out.

'Well, I always thought that's what you wanted; that's what your mother said.'

I looked at my gran's hat and coat hanging on the back of the kitchen door.

'No I didn't,' my mum said, squeezing her thumbs. I knew she was crying. 'I love this house. This is my home; it has a lot of memories.'

'A lot of rows,' my grandad said. 'What about you?' He reached across the table and touched my hand, making me jump.

'More good than bad,' my mum blew her nose. 'A lot of happy times.' She turned around and her eyes were all watery.

'Well, what about you?' Grandad asked again.

'What do you mean?' I said, but I knew what he meant.

'Do you want to live with your aunty Enid and your uncle Mike or do you want to stay with your mum?'

I stood up and felt dizzy like when I used to put my gran's glasses on. 'My mum,' I said, 'I think.'

'Well, it's up to you.' Then he shouted after my mum as she slammed the door. 'You'll have to mend your ways now,' and quietly to himself, 'she should have been drowned at birth.'

'Just pull over by that van, will you?' my mum said to the taxi driver. The white van reflected the light from the headlights back into the taxi; he dipped them.

'No,' my mum said, 'leave them on, then we can see what we're doing.' He flicked a switch and they came back on again.

The taxi driver took out the suitcases and lined them up on the pavement.

''I'll get these,' my mum said, getting in front of him to take her dresses off the back seat. 'Can you give us a hand with these?' She looked at the house to show him where we had to go.

'Me, leave my cab?' the taxi driver said and shook his head. 'Round here, not likely.'

'I won't be a minute then,' my mum said. 'I'll have to get my purse.' We carried two cases each; Mum's dresses were draped over her shoulders.

'I told you it's not very big and it needs a bit of doing up but it's all right,' she said, opening the door. 'Go in, I'll see to the taxi driver.' I tried the light switch but the light didn't come on. From the light in the hall I could see into the room. I went over to the window. My mum was talking to the taxi driver; suddenly it looked like an argument. He jabbed her with his finger, then he walked round to the driver's side of the car, got in, opened the other door on my mother's side and she got in. At first I thought they were going to drive away, then he switched off the headlights. After about ten minutes the car door opened, my mum got out, smoothed down her skirt and walked quickly towards the house.

'What are you doing in the dark?' she said when she came in.

'It doesn't work,' I said. 'What were you doing?'

'It's the meter,' she said, picking up a jar of coins by the door. 'It needs feeding again and this won't last long.' The light came on.

'What were you doing?' I asked again and looked around. 'Is this it then?'

'Poor man,' she said, bringing a suitcase in from the hallway. 'He wanted to talk to somebody; he's got a lot of problems.'

'I think you'd better give this room a good talking to,' I said.

She had nailed a clothes line the length of one wall for all her dresses. I had my own 'wardrobe' on another wall.

'Now I'm going to make us a nice cup of coffee.' She went behind a purple curtain, then stuck out her head. 'And the next item is a cup of coffee, a cup of coffee.' I sat by the electric fire and waited.

'I'm sorry,' my mum said, sitting down beside me. 'I forgot to get some milk.'

'Never mind,' I said, 'I'll get some tomorrow.' I carefully sipped the coffee.

'Is it all right?' my mum asked.

'Yes, it's fine,' I said, but all I could taste was my mum's perfume.

'What's in there?' I said, pointing at a curtain that looked as if it was made out of onion bags.

'Ziz,' my mum said, slowly pulling it back, 'is ze master bedroom; this is yours.'

'Where's your bed?' I said, looking round for another curtain.

'Here,' she said, patting the back of a sofa. 'Cosy, isn't it?'

'I wish I had a flame thrower.' She came and sat next to me, but I moved away.

'I know it's not great,' she said, 'but it's a start. You should have seen some of the places I looked at.' She moved closer to me but I didn't want her to touch me.

I didn't sleep much that first night but I must have slept because I dreamt about my gran and woke up crying: Gran, I miss you so much. Gran, I miss you. I wanted my own bedroom, my own pillow, my own smells and sounds. I listened but it was all far away and strange. My mum started snoring.

*

I stopped going to school and saved the bus fare my mum gave me. It took me about twenty minutes to walk into town; the Central Library was always warm, it had a coffee, hot chocolate and soup machine. I used to switch the labels around so that when people used it they didn't get what they wanted. I sat nearby pretending to read. Usually they drank it anyway but sometimes they just took a sip, left it on the windowsill and went to complain. I drank a lot of coffee, hot chocolate and soup.

One day I picked up a magazine called *House and Garden* and began to read it and look at the pictures. Then I read it again and looked round for some more.

When I got home I took the magazines out of my shirt and started to cut the pictures out. I pinned them all over the room, on the windows, floors, I even got up to the ceiling. My mum came in just as I had finished. I could see she was tired and wanted to go to bed.

'Sit down here,' I said, pulling a chair to the centre of the room for her. 'Listen, this is how I'm going to do it up.' I stood by the wall. 'All the walls are grey,' I stretched my arms out, 'like this.' I showed her the picture: 'Dark blue doors and the skirting-board and here,' I ran to the fire, 'a big square white fireplace. Look, here's a picture and this mirror . . .' I gave it to my mum, 'that goes over the white fireplace and here opposite each other two white sofas, here and here. The company's called . . .' I checked, 'Lebus. Instead of curtains, what do you call them? You know, they go up and down, rollo blinds, with this design.' I drew the Greek key pattern. 'A long table like this,' I walked the length and turned, 'and ten chairs and flowers, big blue flowers and nothing else.' Then I remembered the ceiling and I pointed. 'Dark blue and a light, a big round light that comes right down to here.' I held my hands just above where the table would be.

'What else? The carpet ... grey, plain grey like the walls and between the sofas a white rug and by the fire-place two stone lions.' I searched the room.

'It'll cost a fortune,' my mum said, looking at the pictures. 'I can't afford all this.'

'But you said we could do it up,' I said.

'I know,' she said, giving back the pictures, 'but ...'

'We can do it a bit at a time,' I said, 'not all at once.'

'I couldn't afford this, not in a month of Sundays,' my mum said taking off her coat, putting it on a hanger and hanging it up. 'I mean, I can just about pay the rent and I'm a bit behind with that.'

I picked up a magazine and turned the pages. 'You've always got money for clothes,' I said, looking past her at the line of dresses hanging on the wall.

'Second-hand,' she said. 'I haven't bought anything new for years, except my knickers and bras. This lot isn't worth more than twenty quid and some of it's still on tick.'

I rolled up the magazine and threw it across the room and walked out slamming the door behind me.

My mum opening the door woke me up.

'Shhh,' I heard my mum whisper. 'No, don't put the light on. Wait a minute, let me get my coat off.' I was wide awake, and I took the knife out from under my pillow.

'There's nothing behind the curtain, come here,' my mum said.

They stopped talking but I could hear them. A match was struck and I held my breath.

'No, you can't stay,' my mum whispered, 'and you can smoke that when you get outside.'

'Who says I'm going,' I heard a man say.

'Shhh, I say so. My landlord's just next door. You don't want me to get thrown out, do you?' He said something but I couldn't make out what it was. 'Come on,' my mum said, 'don't be greedy, there's a good boy.'

She opened the door and pushed the man out.

'Bitch,' he said and slapped her.

'Who was that?' I said from behind the curtain.

'I know who he wasn't,' she said, dabbing her lip with her handkerchief.

'Who?' She switched on a new lamp and looked in my direction. 'Who?' I said again.

'Who, who, you sound like an owl.'

'You said you know who he wasn't.'

'It wasn't Gary Cooper, I know that,' she said, looking down at the crumpled one pound note in her hand. 'God knows . . . A nutter . . . As usual . . .'

'Does it hurt?'

'It will in the morning,' she said, checking the pound note against the lamplight. 'Shit, that's all I need, a fat lip when I'm going away . . .' She glanced quickly at the curtain. 'It's a special job. It's only for a few days. There's no money around just now.' She moved closer to the curtain. 'Too many at it, it's always the same just before Christmas. You'll be all right, won't you?' Her nose almost touching the curtain. 'Won't you? I'll be back for Christmas . . . I don't want to go . . . You know that, don't you? But Christmas is coming and . . . Oh . . . Sod Christmas . . . Christmas or no Christmas, we need some money.' She sighed.

'But I'm getting too old for this and it's getting harder to find. I don't know where to turn, I don't know what I'm going to do.' She looked at the blood on her hand-kerchief.

'If I could, I'd get a job,' she said suddenly as if answering a question. 'But what could I do? I couldn't get a job and doing what? And who would give me a job? There's this old man . . .' She laughed . . .

'Says he wants to take care of me. He's sort of . . . crippled. His legs are all twisted. We'd make a handsome couple, wouldn't we? No, I'd rather beg and that's it, it's come to that . . . And I had such big ideas . . . I was going to be different . . . well, this is different all right. When I was young I thought I knew it all, nobody could tell me . . . I wouldn't listen. I wish I'd listened now. I wish I could go back and start again, I'd do things different . . . And I was clever too, just as clever as you are. I was always top of the class and I wasn't even trying. One of my teachers, Miss Wood, wanted me to take some special exams . . . But all I was interested in was dressing up and going out . . . pictures, dancing and boyfriends. I've wasted my life, I could have made something of myself. I could have been anything, instead of . . .

'I once had a job, I mean a real one, you know; in fact I've had two but I don't think the first one counted because I never got paid and it only lasted about a quarter of an hour. I was a waitress, I'm not having people snapping their fingers at me. Then I got a job working in an ice cream factory making ice lollies. It was horrible, but it was either that or the land army. It was just before the end of the war and there were foreign soldiers everywhere. I was walking home from work when this big car stopped and this man – a soldier, a Yank – offered me a lift. "Hey kid, save your legs, get in." When I got in he said he hadn't seen me around before and I told him I hadn't seen him before either, so what? Then I twigged what he was going on about . . . there were always some girls standing near the station working, you know . . . And he thought I was one of them. He took me for a drink. I remember I had to keep my gloves on because I'd been working on lime ice lollies all day and my hands were bright green. When we got back into the car he offered me some money; well, it was more than a week's wages, so I took it and I never went back to Ronaldo's ices. I was making plenty of money then and spending it too. I used to buy things for your gran but she would never take anything. I once bought her a dinner service, plates, cups, saucers, everything in a big box with a big bow. I left it for her on the kitchen table . . . The next day I found it in the dustbin all smashed up . . .

'If I could go back just ten years and know what I know now . . . I'm not old but in this game you get old before your time. I'm looking for somebody a bit younger, they say and drive off. Then it's beggars can't be choosers and you start doing it with the likes of that one. Not that you remember any of them; perhaps the first one or two you do but after that, why would you want to remember? No thank you, you'd want to forget. And people think it's easy to get out. What do they know? It's a lot easier to get in. When I was young I used to laugh at the old ones standing around in the freezing rain . . . Poor cows, I'd say; that'll never happen to me.'

Winter came without warning. I woke up and all the windows inside were covered in ice. I hadn't seen my mum for about a week and there was only a shilling left in the jar. I'd been banned from the library but I knew a few shops where I could get some crisps and a Mars bar or something. I was good at nicking things. Then I got caught. I was just making up my mind between a Bounty and a Kit Kat when I saw the shopkeeper watching me in a mirror. I didn't run, I just walked out of the shop and I thought I'd got away with it when all of a sudden – *bang* – he's got me pinned up against the wall.

'Right, you little bugger, let's see what you've got this time.' He found a bag of crisps inside my anorak and hit me in the face with them.

'What's he done?' a man asked with a silly grin on his face.

'Nicking,' the shopkeeper said, ripping both pockets off my anorak.

'Well, don't be too rough. Look, his nose is bleeding.'

'I've a good mind to give him some more,' he said, lifting me off the ground. 'He's done me every day this week but I was ready for him this time.'

'I bought them, honest, I bought them,' I tried.

'Look, you go and phone the police,' silly grin said, 'and I'll hold him.'

'Right, I won't be a minute, thanks.' And he ran back to the shop. Then silly grin let go of my arm.

'Go on,' he said, 'go on, get lost.' I thought it was some sort of trick, so I didn't move; then he pushed me. 'Sod off.' And he smiled. 'Run, before he comes back.'

I stayed indoors for a couple of days. I was warm because I stayed in bed but I was hungry. I thought I'd risk the library again. I was just about to leave when I heard somebody pushing something under the door. It was a letter and I recognized the handwriting. It was from Mrs Didimsky asking for her rent, so I didn't open it.

The library was closed; it was the day before Christmas day and all the shops had their decorations up. I stopped to look at the watches in H. Samuel. I felt somebody leaning against my back.

'Nice, aren't they?'

I turned around and it was an old man and he was smiling. 'They're all right,' I said and moved away. I'd seen him around. The card in the window said: BETTINA THE SLIMMEST WATCH IN THE WORLD. I tried to see just how slim it was and banged my head against the window.

'Ouch,' the old man said, starting to lean again. 'Is that what you're getting for Christmas?'

'No,' I said, taking a step sideways. 'I've already got one.'

'See that?' The old man pulled back his cuff to show off his watch. 'Twenty-four carat, twenty-one jewe . . .'

I was half-way across the road and I could see his reflection in the shop window. He was following me.

'You're not English, are you?' he said.

'I am,' I looked back over my shoulder at him.

'You look foreign to me . . . a bit mysterious.'

I stopped and looked at him. 'Look . . .' I started. I was going to tell him to fuck off; I knew what he was after.

'I was just about to have lunch . . .' He took a deep breath. 'Would you care to join me? I'll pay.' He didn't have to ask twice.

'This is my nephew,' the old man said to the Italian waiter. It didn't seem strange; my mum used to say things like that all the time.

'It's good to see a young person with such a good appetite,' he said, pouring me a glass of wine. 'Go on, wash it down with that . . . liquid sunshine. Oh, how I love the Mediterranean . . . Have you travelled much?' He poured me another glass of wine. 'Here, finish this,' he said, sliding his steak off his plate onto mine. 'I have no appetite these days.'

'South of France,' I said and tore into the new steak. 'I go every year with my mum.'

'St Tropez, Cannes, Nice, the Côte d'Azure. Sunshine, Heaven's golden eye,' he said.

'I'll have your chips too if you don't want them,' I said.

My face was hot and I felt a bit sick as I followed the old man up the stairs to his flat.

'Yes, it's a very nice restaurant,' he went on, 'but I know they serve instant coffee and I make the real thing. Come in. Welcome.'

The room was large with a big sofa covered in a pink and purple shawl. One wall was filled with books; there were religious pictures on the other walls.

'Do you like art?' the old man said, lighting the gas fire.

'It's all right,' I said. 'I feel a bit sick.'

'Strong black coffee espresso will do the trick.' The old man held my hot face with his cold hands. 'I'll go and change first.'

I opened the door and went and stood on the balcony. I could hear him singing. He asked me to choose a record but I was too busy trying to hold on to my lunch. I couldn't stop it. First the wine sprayed out of my nose.

'Would you like some cognac with your coffee?' he shouted from the bedroom.

'No,' I squeaked and it was all over – all over the balcony below.

'Oh dear,' he said, standing behind me. He was wearing a silk robe. 'Come and sit down, you poor thing. I'll get you some water and a towel. Perhaps you'd better put your feet up; I'll take your shoes.'

*

82

It was getting dark when I woke up and the old man was lying beside me on the sofa, looking at me and stroking my hair.

'Feeling better?' he asked. I could smell the wine on his breath as he tried to kiss me.

'I have to go,' I said, getting up from the sofa. 'Where's my jeans?'

'Don't go,' he said and grabbed my arm. 'Let me hold you, I just want to hold you,' and he pulled me back on to the sofa. 'Beautiful you are, beautiful, I just want to hold you.' He put his arms around me and gripped me with his knees. 'Beautiful.'

'I want to go home,' I said, struggling to get free and dodging his kisses. 'I'm late.'

Then he suddenly let go and sent me sprawling backwards against a chair.

'I want my jeans,' I said, getting up and getting behind the chair.

'You're not going anywhere,' he said, going over to the fire.

'Let me go,' I said, and looked at all the locks on the door.

'I can't let my friends down can I?' he said. 'They're on their way now. I just phoned them, they can't wait to meet you. But first I've got to teach you a lesson, some respect.' He started towards me.

'I want to go,' I shouted, moving back and pulling the chair with me.

'Shout all you like, nobody will hear you. Now, I want you to be nice to my friends, do you understand?' He made a grab for me but missed. I got behind the sofa. 'Calm down,' he said, coming for me again. 'Relax.' A cold breeze blew across my legs. The balcony door was still open. He saw me look at it and tried to stop me, but I was too fast. I climbed over the balcony rail and held on, crouching like in a racing dive, and stared into the branches of a tree. The uppermost branches reached towards the balcony, offering some hope. I knew I could make it.

'What are you doing?' The old man froze. 'Don't be silly,' he said. 'Come on, I'll let you go, honest.'

I looked back at him over my shoulder.

'Trust me, come back in. Come on. You can't fly.'

I took a deep breath, and it was my best dive ever.